The ...

Tenali ...

Compiled by Mrs Rungeen Singh

Young Learner Publications™

G-1, Rattan Jyoti,
18, Rajendra Place
New Delhi-110008 (INDIA)
Ph.: 25750801, 25820556
Fax : 91-11-25764396

Printed at : Kumar Offset Printers, Delhi-110092

CONTENTS

TENALI RAMAN

In a South Indian village called Tenali, there lived a clever Brahmin boy named Raman. He was a very good looking young boy.

A wandering holy man saw him and took an instant liking to him. The learned holy man taught Raman a chant.

The holy man told Raman, “If you go to Goddess Kali’s temple at night and recite this chant three million times, the Goddess will appear before you.”

Raman asked, “How will I recognise her?”

The holy man replied, “The Goddess has one thousand heads.”

Raman asked, “What should I do then?”

The holy man said, “You can ask her for anything. She will give you what you ask for, but only if you don’t get scared of her.”

Raman then had a bath and went to the temple, and started chanting.

Just as he completed the chant three million times, the Goddess appeared before him.

Raman looked at her and started laughing. He laughed and laughed and laughed.

The Goddess became very angry but Raman went on laughing.

Then the Goddess said, “You are laughing at me. I curse you that throughout your life, you will remain a joker and others will laugh at you.”

Raman still kept on laughing.

The Goddess asked, “I have cursed you, yet you continue to laugh. Why?”

Raman said, “We humans, have one nose and two hands, and when we have a cold, we suffer so much.”

The Goddess asked, “So?”

Raman said, “You have thousand noses. I wonder, how you'll manage if you catch cold?”

The Goddess smiled at this. Then she looked at Raman and said, “You have a good sense of humour. I have already cursed you, and I can't take it back.”

The Goddess continued, “I will make it better by blessing you that you will earn money as a royal jester.”

When Tenali Raman grew up, this curse turned into a blessing.

He always kept King Krishnadev Rai of Vijaynagar in a good mood with his wit.

THE COLOURED BIRD

One day, a bird catcher came to the court of King Krishnadev Rai. He had a very beautiful coloured bird with him.

The man said, "I have caught this bird especially for you. It is a rare bird. Just see its beautiful colours, My Lord."

The king said, "Yes, I have never seen such a wonderful and colourful bird. It is really beautiful."

The man continued, "This bird can talk like a parrot and dance like a peacock."

The king was very fond of birds and animals. He was very happy to add such a wonderful bird to his royal garden.

He said to his minister, "Give fifty gold coins to this man as reward for bringing such a lovely bird."

As the bird catcher was about to leave, Tenali Raman got up and said, "My Lord, I don't think that this bird can dance like a peacock in the rain."

The man asked, "How can you say so?"

Tenali Raman asked him, "Have you ever given this bird a bath? I don't think so. I feel it has not been bathed for a long time."

"What are you trying to say," said the puzzled man.

"Just wait and watch," said Tenali.

Saying this, Tenali got up and brought a jug full of water. He poured the water on the coloured bird.

The water drained the colour from the bird's body. The bird had now began to look like any other ordinary bird.

The king said, “What! This colour is not natural. Has it been painted on the bird.”

Tenali Raman said, “It is just an ordinary pigeon, My Lord. This man has painted it.”

The king asked, “But how did you know that this bird was painted? Tenali Raman, tell us.”

Tenali Raman said, “I saw his coloured nails. My Lord, his nails are still stained with the colours he had used on the pigeon.”

The king looked at the hands of the bird catcher. His nails still had some paint on them.

Caught red-handed, the man tried to run away but the guards caught him. The bird catcher was sent to prison.

The king was glad that Tenali Raman had saved him from being cheated.

The money which was to be given to the man with the coloured bird, was then rewarded to Tenali Raman.

THE KING'S FACE

Tenali Raman came to the court one day and to his utter surprise, he saw the king giving each courtier a bag of gold coins.

All the courtiers looked happy as they took the money.

The king announced, "You have to spend all this money within a week's time. The unspent money will have to be returned to the royal treasury."

They all shouted with joy, "Thank you, Your Highness."

Their joy was short lived for the king said, "However, you must see my face before you buy anything with this money."

The courtiers did not know what to do. They wanted to spend the money but they could not. How could they come to see the king's face every time they went to buy something?

They could not disturb the king every time they wanted to buy something. He would get angry.

Some courtiers felt that the king had kept this condition to make sure that none of them could spend the money.

When one week was over, all of them came to the court. The first thing the king asked was, "What did you buy with the money I had given you?"

All the courtiers looked at each other. They were unhappy as they had not been able to buy anything with the money.

The courtiers came one by one and returned the bag of gold to the king.

They said, "We could not buy anything because how could we see your face every time we went for shopping?"

When Tenali Raman came to the court, the king asked him, "Are you not returning the money?"

Tenali Raman replied, "I have bought many things and I spent all the money on the first day itself."

The courtiers thought that the king would be angry because Tenali Raman had spent all the money without seeing the face of the king.

An angry courtier remarked, "Did the king go with you to the market? Is that how you saw his face?"

Tenali Raman replied, "The king did not have to be there. On every golden coin there is the face of the king. I saw that and bought things. Thank you, My Lord, I have bought many things and my family is very happy and thankful to you."

Pleased with Tenali's clever thinking and wit, the king gave him another bag of coins as reward.

THE DEBT SICKNESS

Once Tenali Raman did not attend the court for three days. He sent a message to the king saying that he was very sick.

The king went to Tenali Raman's house to wish him a speedy recovery.

When the king saw Tenali Raman lying covered with a blanket, he realised that Tenali Raman was really sick.

The king asked Tenali Raman's wife, "How has he become sick?"

She replied, "My Lord, he has to pay you the money he borrowed from you. This worry has made him sick."

The king replied, "If that is the reason, then forget about the debt. You don't have to pay that money back to me."

Actually Tenali Raman was not sick at all. He did not want to return the money he had borrowed from the king, so he pretended to be very sick.

The moment Tenali Raman heard the king waiving off his debt, Tenali threw the blanket aside and jumped up from the bed. He thanked the king but the king got very angry when he realised that Tenali was feigning his illness.

The king shouted, "So you are not sick. You were trying to fool me, Tenali Raman."

Tenali Raman said, "No, My Lord. I was sick due to the burden of your debt. But now that the debt is removed, I am well again. The sickness has disappeared on its own."

The king smiled at his wit.

THE STOLEN BRINJALS

King Krishnadev Rai loved to eat good food. He was very fond of brinjals and he had the gardener plant some wonderful brinjals in the royal garden.

The king did not permit anyone but the royal gardener to go near the brinjals.

There were guards all around the brinjal garden so that no one could steal them.

One day, when the king was having his meal, he gave some cooked brinjal to Tenali to eat. Tenali found the dish very delicious.

He went home and told his wife how tasty the brinjals had been. The way Tenali discribed the taste of the king's brinjals, his wife's mouth began to water. She insisted that he should bring some brinjals for her too.

Tenali Raman said, "The king guards these brinjals as he guards his crown. How can I get them for you?"

Tenali Raman's wife became angry.

She insisted, "I don't know. I want those brinjals and you have to get them."

Unable to convince his wife, Tenali Raman then went in the middle of the night and scaled the wall of the king's vegetable garden.

He made sure that the guards did not see him. He quickly plucked some ripe brinjals and tied them in a piece of cloth.

He then took them home to his wife.

His wife prepared a tasty dish with the brinjals and served the dish for dinner. His wife loved the brinjals and relished every bite of it.

Suddenly his wife said, “Oh! Our son has not eaten his dinner. He too loves brinjals. He should also eat these delicious brinjals. He is sleeping on the terrace. Please go and call him.”

Tenali Raman said, “He is a child. He might go and tell others that the brinjals were from the king’s garden. Let him sleep. He should not know that we have eaten brinjals for dinner.”

But his wife would not listen. Unable to convince his wife, Tenali Raman went upstairs. He took a bucket full of water and sprinkled some water all around the bed on the floor.

He then poured the water on his son who woke up with a start.

Tenali said to his son, “Come on, son. It is raining. Let us go downstairs.”

The sleepy boy got up and started walking downstairs.

As he was walking, Tenali Raman poured some more water on his son's head and said, "Hurry up, son. It is raining really hard."

They reached down and the boy was fed brinjals which he really enjoyed. Soon after the meal they all went to sleep.

Next morning, the gardener found out that some brinjals had been stolen from the garden.

The gardener rushed to the prime minister and told him about the stolen brinjals. The prime minister thought that it could only be Tenali Raman. He went and told the king.

The king said, "That can be true, but if you ask Tenali then he will use his wit to save himself. Go and ask his son instead to find out the truth."

So, Tenali Raman's son was brought to the court.

The king very softly asked, "What did you have for dinner last night?"

The boy said, “Oh! We had brinjals My Lord, and they tasted very good.”

The king was convinced that Tenali had stolen the brinjals. He turned to Tenali and said, “So you have stolen the brinjals from my garden.”

Tenali said, "My Lord, this boy is always daydreaming. Please ask him about the weather yesterday."

The king asked Tenali's son, "What was the weather like yesterday?"

The son said, "It rained a lot at night."

The king looked at the prime minister who said, "No, child. It did not rain."

But the child insisted, "Of course, it rained very heavily. I got all wet."

Tenali Raman then said, "Yesterday it did not rain. You all know that. My son must have dreamt that it was raining and he was eating brinjals."

The king was convinced that Tenali was speaking the truth and that his son had actually been daydreaming.

The king felt sorry that he had accused Tenali of stealing the brinjals.

The king and the prime minister apologised to Tenali Raman, and the king gave wonderful gifts to his son.

THE BARBER MINISTER

The barber who used to shave King Krishnadev Rai was very good at his work.

One day, when he came to give a shave to the king, he found the king sleeping. The barber, not wanting to disturb the king's sleep, quietly shaved the king's beard and went away.

When the king woke up, he was surprised that the barber had shaved him while he slept. He thought that the barber was really very good and should be rewarded for this.

Pleased with his workmanship, the king called him and said, “This is wonderful. How can you shave a sleeping man without disturbing his sleep? Ask me and I will give you whatever you want.”

Hesitantly the barber said, “My Lord, please make me a minister. I have always dreamt to be one.”

The king immediately issued orders for the barber to be made a minister of the court.

Tenali Raman was not present that day. All the ministers got together and held a meeting. They were not ready to accept an uneducated man like the barber in their midst.

They wondered as to how could an uneducated person, with no previous experience, be appointed as a minister.

They had lengthy discussions, but no one could muster the courage to tell the king that his decision to appoint the barber a minister was not right.

So, they all agreed to go to Tenali Raman to seek his advice. They were sure that he would surely find a solution.

One minister said to Tenali Raman, "You must do something otherwise any uneducated common person can become a minister in the court. Then what will be our importance."

Tenali assured the ministers, "Don't worry. I will do something. All you have to do is to bring the king to the river side tomorrow evening."

When the king came walking near the river, he was surprised to see Tenali Raman scrubbing a black dog.

The king asked, "Tenali, why are you scrubbing this dog so hard?"

Tenali said, "I want to change his black colour to white, My Lord!"

The king said, “He has been born as a black dog. How can you make him white? Now stop acting foolish.”

Tenali said, “Why My Lord? When an uneducated person like a barber can become a minister then why can't this black dog be turned into white?”

The king did not say anything and walked away, lost in deep thought. Next day, the king called the barber minister and said, “I can make you the minister on the condition that you will have to study and educate yourself. Till then I take back my order issued yesterday.”

THE KING'S REWARD

Once there lived a poor man in a very small hut. He was so poor that he did not even have enough money to buy his food.

One day the poor man gathered courage to go to the court and ask the king for help.

The man said, “My Lord, I do not have money to buy even food. Can you help me?”

But even before the king could say anything, the head priest came forward and asked the man not to trouble the king, and sent him away. The priest was very greedy and did not want the king to give money to anyone but the priest.

The poor man went back disappointed. Outside the court, a kind minister advised him to approach Tenali Raman for help. The poor man went to Tenali Raman and narrated his story.

Tenali Raman said, “You go back and don’t worry. I will definitely do something for you. After two days, just go to the forest in the morning, and come back to your hut later in the day.”

Tenali prepared a plan to help the poor man. Tenali knew that the king had already planned to visit a holy man in the forest. He accompanied the king to the forest along with the royal priest and some guards.

He guided the king through a longer route to the hut of the holy man. As a result the king got tired and started feeling hungry.

They decided to stop and have lunch. As they sat down for lunch, Tenali cleverly spilled all the water from the jar.

No one realised that he had done that intentionally.

The food was tasty but very spicy. The king asked for water as soon as he had finished his meal. But there was no water left. The guards looked around but could not find any well.

Tenali took this opportunity and took them to a nearby hut. There was no one inside the hut. Tenali gave water to the king from a pot in the hut.

As the king was drinking water, a man came in and said, "This is my hut. What are you all doing here?" This was the same poor man.

But as the poor man saw the king he folded his hands with respect.

The king said, “I was very thirsty and drank water from your pot. Now, you can ask for anything.”

The royal priest immediately interrupted and said, “My Lord, give him a few gold coins.”

Tenali said, "My Lord! Our priest says things without thinking."

The king asked, "What are you trying to say Tenali Raman?"

Tenali said, "This is an important day. It will be written down in books of history."

The priest asked, "What do you mean?"

Tenali answered, "The people would discuss that the great King Krishnadev Rai stopped for lunch in the forest and had water from a poor man's hut."

"So?" asked the priest.

Tenali said, "They would also talk about the reward that the poor man was given by the king."

Before the priest could say anything, the king removed a very costly necklace from around his neck and gave it to the poor man.

The king and the others then walked away towards their horses.

The poor man folded his hands and thanked Tenali Raman.

ELEPHANTS OR COWS

Once King Krishnadev Rai was so pleased with the wit of Tenali Raman that he gifted him five elephants as a token of appreciation.

Tenali knew that the elephants would be of no use to him but he could not gather the courage to refuse the gift.

He thanked the king and took the elephants home.

When he reached home, his wife got very very angry with poor Tenali.

She shouted, “Why did you take such a gift?”

Tenali said, “How could I refuse a gift from the king?”

His wife said, “We do not have enough to feed our children. How will we feed five elephants?”

Tenali said, “What can I do?”

His wife said, “Had the king gifted five cows, it would have helped us. We could have given the cows’ milk to our children.”

Tenali knew that his wife was right. He thought and thought, and soon came up with an idea. He took the five elephants to the middle of the city and left them there and came back home.

The hungry elephants roamed around the city and if someone took pity on the elephants he would feed them, otherwise they would remain hungry.

In a few day's time, the elephants became very weak.

One day some jealous courtiers went to the king and informed him that Tenali was not looking after the elephants which the king had gifted to him.

The king became very angry and called Tenali to the court. He asked Tenali the reason for his negligence.

Tenali Raman bowed to the king and said, "My Lord. I have a large family to look after. I do not have sufficient money to feed my family membes then how can I feed the elephants?"

The king said, "I don't agree with you. Why didn't you tell me then? I would have rewarded you something else."

Tenali said, "Had I refused the gift it would have been an insult to you. You would have been angry and rightly so."

The king was beginning to realise his mistake.

Tenali added, "My Lord, only kings can afford elephants as pets. An ordinary person like me cannot afford to look after them. If you had given me cows instead, they would have been more useful. We could have given their milk to our children."

The king was convinced that it had not been wise on his part to gift elephants to Tenali.

But he said, "Had I given you cows, you would not have looked after them either."

Tenali said, "Cows give us milk. I could have given the milk to my children to drink and sold the excess milk. Also My Lord, cows do not eat as much as elephants. I could have cared for them very well."

The king ordered his men that the elephants be taken back from Tenali Raman, and instead five cows be given to him.

The cows were immediately sent to Tenali's house.

Tenali's wife was glad to have the cows. The cows proved to be very useful. They gave milk which Tenali's children gladly drank. Tenali's wife sold the excess milk and was able to buy many things. She looked after the cows very well.

THEFT OF THE FLOWERS

King Krishnadev Rai was once gifted a beautiful rose plant by a close friend.

The rose creeper grew well and very soon spread all over the high walls of his palace.

In the flowering season, lovely roses bloomed. The king loved the beautiful roses and told his gardener to make sure that no one plucked them.

One day, the king called his gardener.

He said, "Look! For the past few days I have noticed that someone is stealing the roses. Their number is decreasing every day."

The gardener asked the king to position a guard to secretly watch the garden. So, a guard was posted and the thief was caught the very next day. He had his hands full of roses. He was none other than the ten year old son of Tenali Raman.

In those days, it was a custom to parade the thief throughout the city. This served two purposes. One, the people would come to know who the thief was and at the same time the thief would also be ashamed of his misdeed.

Tenali Raman's son was also taken around the city in the same way.

When they passed Tenali's house, his wife saw her son with the guard.

She was shocked and shouted out to Tenali who also came out to see.

Tenali and his wife tried to speak to their son but the guard did not allow them to meet.

Tenali's wife started crying and asked Tenali to help their son.

She cried, "Why don't you do something for your son? You are so close to the king. Please ask the guard to forgive him."

Tenali said loudly, "I can't do that. Our son has got into trouble. He should use his mouth to get out of this."

The son heard this and felt bad that even his father was not ready to help him.

But suddenly he realised what his father was trying to say. The son understood what his father wanted to tell him. He had to use his mouth!

The mouth is used to talk and also to eat. Tenali's son started eating the roses.

By the time they reached the king, the son had eaten all the roses, without the guard realising it.

The guard produced him before the king. He told the king that he had caught Tenali's son red-handed, stealing the roses from the garden.

"This small boy cannot be the thief," said the king, not believing the guard.

The guard tried in vain to convince the king that Tenali Raman's son was indeed the thief.

The boy said, "My Lord, I was just passing that way and this man caught me. I am innocent."

The guard lost his temper and said, "No, My Lord, he is lying. I caught him red-handed near the rose creeper while he was plucking the flowers."

The son said, "My Lord, he has failed to catch the real culprit and so has framed me."

The guard shouted angrily, "Don't tell lies."

The boy said, "If I had stolen the roses, they should have been in my hands. But see there are no roses in my hands."

The king saw the empty hands of the boy. He got very angry with the guard for trying to frame a small innocent child.

The boy was set free but he had learnt his lesson that stealing was not the right thing to do. He pledged never to take anything that did not belong to him. Not even a flower!

TENALI AND CHESS

Tenali Raman did not know how to play chess. He did not even enjoy watching other people play the game.

One day, when Tenali was not there, a courtier said to the king, "My Lord, why don't you play chess? You are so good at it."

The king said, "There is no one good enough to play chess with me, so I have given up playing the game."

Some of the courtiers, who were jealous of Tenali Raman, wanted to show Tenali down.

One of them said, "But My Lord, you have such a good chess player in your court."

"Whom are you talking about?" asked the king.

"Tenali Raman, My Lord! He plays chess very well," said the courtier.

The king was surprised and said, "But whenever I have asked him to play, he has always refused saying that he does not know how to play chess."

The courtier said, "He likes to play chess alone. Maybe that is why he has lied to you that he does not play chess."

The king said, "If that is so, let him come to the court tomorrow, I will force him to play chess with me."

Next day whenTenali Raman came to the court, he saw the king sitting with a chess board in front of him.

The king ordered, "Tenali, come let us play."

Tenali replied, "My Lord, I am sorry. I don't know how to play chess."

The courtier excitedly said, "Your secret is out Tenali. Now the king knows that you can play chess."

Tenali Raman immediately realised that the jealous courtiers wanted to show him down in front of the king.

So, he quietly sat down. The king started playing. Tenali had no idea what to do. He just moved his pieces here and there.

This made the king angry. He said, "Tenali. Play properly."

Tenali said, "I am playing as properly as I can, My Lord."

The courtier said, "My Lord. Tenali is intentionally playing like a fool. He doesn't want you to know the good moves."

The king lost his patience and shouted, “If you don’t play properly Tenali, I will have your hair shaved off.”

Poor Tenali. No matter how hard he tried, all his moves were bad; this further angered the king.

By now the king was very angry and he summoned the guards and said, "Go, call the barber and get Tenali's head shaved."

Tenali said, "But My Lord. I have sold my hair for two thousand gold coins to a man. I can't get my hair cut till I pay the man two thousand gold coins."

The angry king ordered for two thousand gold coins to be given to Tenali.

The money was handed over to Tenali. As the barber was about to shave him, Tenali held his hand.

The king shouted, "Now what is it? You have got the two thousand gold coins and it is time for your hair to be shaved off."

Tenali said, "My Lord, in my family, our heads are shaven only when our parents die. My parents are already dead. But you are like a father to me. I hope that when my head is shaved off, nothing bad happens to you."

"Stop! Don't cut his hair," the king ordered.

Then the king asked Tenali, "Be honest, do you know how to play chess?"

Tenali said, "No, My Lord. I don't know how to play chess. But I wish I knew."

"Why?" asked the king.

Tenali said, "I don't know chess and still I got two thousand gold coins from it. If I knew chess, I could have earned much more."

The king and the courtiers had a hearty laugh.

THE CAMEL STORY

Once the king called Tenali Raman and said, "Tenali I am so happy with you that I want to gift you a city."

Tenali Raman was shocked when he heard this. He looked at the king in disbelief and said, “Mmmyyy Lllooord! What did you say just now?”

The king repeated, “Tenali, I am so happy with what you have done, that I want to gift a city to you.”

Tenali’s happiness was widely written on his face. To receive a whole city as a gift from the king, was something he had not even dreamt of.

Now he would be rich and always have enough money. His sons and his wife would be happy too.

He went home and gave the news to his family. They were overjoyed.

Now every day, when he returned home they would ask, “Did the king tell you which city you will get?”

“No. It seems that the king has forgotten his promise,” Tenali would say.

Slowly, everyone in the family started feeling that they would never have the city as promised by the king.

Now, Tenali thought that since the king had forgotten about his promise, he should remind him about it.

However, he could not gather the courage to do this.

One day, an Arab came to their city. He had a camel with him. No one in the kingdom had ever seen a camel before.

The king went with Tenali Raman to see the camel.

The king remarked, "What an ugly animal this is. It has such a long neck."

Tenali agreed, "Yes, My Lord."

"And it has two ugly humps," said the king.

"Yes, my Lord. The hump is to store the water," said Tenali.

"I wonder why did God make such an ugly animal?" said the king.

Tenali said, "This camel must have been a king in his previous life. He must have promised a city to a man and then forgotten about it. So, the God must have turned the king into a camel."

The king burst out laughing and then he said, “Oh Tenali Raman! What a fine way of reminding me. Don't worry. You will get your city.”

The king announced the name of the city in the court next day being gifted to Tenali Raman. Tenali and his family were overjoyed on receiving the gift.

PERFORMERS FROM BABAPUR

Every Dussehra, a group of actors would come to Vijayanagar and perform Ram Leela in front of the king and his people.

Once it so happened that the group expressed its inability to come and perform in the kingdom.

The king felt very sad at this. He used to enjoy the performance of the group and also wanted his people to know about the values Lord Ram stood for.

There were only three days left for the starting date of Ram Leela. It was not possible to arrange for an alternative. The king was very disheartened and said, "Will there be no Ram Leela this year?"

Tenali Raman got up and said, "I know a group which can perform the show very well."

The king asked him to immediately go and call them. Meanwhile the city was decorated and the grounds cleaned for the stage to be set up.

The people of the kingdom were happy. Many people put up stalls for sweets and toys on the ground.

Soon the day of the first performance arrived. The group of actors, comprising mostly of children, put up a brilliant performance for the next nine day.

On the last day of the performance, the king invited the group for a royal dinner at his palace.

All the actors enjoyed the grand feast and later received many gifts and presents from the king.

As they were about to leave, the king asked, “Where is this drama group from?”

Tenali said, “Babapur.”

The king said, “But we don’t have a place called Babapur in our kingdom.”

“Er..., it is er..., near Vijayanagar,” replied Tenali Raman.

The king said, “Why are you stammering Tenali? What is the matter?”

One of the actors spoke up, “My Lord, we belong to your kingdom itself.”

“But Babapur is not in my kingdom,” said the King.

One child said, “We address Tenali Raman as Baba. And he prepared us for the drama in three days time. So we are from Babapur.”

The king said “This is very nice. Tenali, you are good at dramatics too. The drama was really good. I enjoyed the performance very much.”

The king gave a handsome reward to Tenali Raman for his sincere efforts.

THE LOST WELLS

King Krishnadev Rai really cared for his people. He tried to make their life easy.

Once, before the onset of the summer season, he called his chief minister and asked him to have wells dug up throughout his kingdom, so that people could get water easily.

The minister was given a lot of money from the royal treasury to get the work done quickly.

Soon, the minister got the wells ready. He took the king around the city for a survey of the wells.

The king was very happy to see that the whole city had enough wells to provide sufficient water to his people.

After a few days some people came from remote villages. They complained to Tenali about the chief minister. They informed him that there were no wells dug up in their villages.

Tenali Raman asked them to come to the court next day.

Tenali said to the king, “My Lord, there are some thieves who are stealing the wells from the ground.”

The king said, “Tenali! Have you gone crazy? How can someone steal a well?”

Tenali said, “But it’s true, My Lord. I have some villagers here with me. Many wells have been stolen from their village.”

The villagers came forward and said, “The wells are not there. They have vanished.”

The king went with the villagers to their villages and was shocked to see that no wells had been dug up there.

The king looked angrily at the chief minister. The minister got very scared.

Tenali said, “My Lord. Please don’t blame the chief minister. The wells have been stolen. It is not his fault.”

“No, Tenali. The wells have not been dug at all. This minister got some wells dug around the city to please me. He did not have wells dug all over the kingdom, as I had asked him to,” the king said.

He turned to the chief minister and said, “Where is the rest of the money I gave you?”

“I have spent it,” said the scared minister.

The king said, “That is your problem now. You have to get the other wells dug with your own money. Tenali Raman will supervise to ensure that you get all the wells dug in time before the summers begin, otherwise you will be punished.”

DYE FOR SWEETS

King Krishnadev Rai was very fond of festivities. Once he declared the next festival to be celebrated in a grand and colourful manner.

The whole city was cleaned up. The houses were decorated with flowers and lights. The palace was looking beautiful.

The king asked the sweet sellers to make colourful sweets as they would look very attractive.

The sweet sellers started making sweets of all colours. Indeed, the sweets looked lovely.

The people wore grand clothes and came to the court, but Tenali Raman was not there. He did not even bother to inform the king of his whereabouts.

The king was worried and asked his guards to look for Tenali Raman.

One of the guards came and reported, "Tenali Raman has set up a dye shop and is busy dyeing clothes for the people."

The king asked, "Did you ask him to come to the court?"

"We did, but he refused," said the guard.

The king got very angry. He shouted, "Tell Tenali to come to the court immediately and if he refuses, get him forcibly."

The guards again went to Tenali Raman but he would not move from his place.

When he refused to come, the guards picked him up and produced him before the king.

The king was holding court when Tenali was brought in.

The king shouted, "You are a royal jester. Why are you not present in the court? Why did you not come when I sent for you? How dare you disobey my orders? You could have done the dyeing work later. What was the urgency?"

Tenali said, "My Lord, I was dyeing the clothes for the festival."

The king asked, "But why didn't you come when you were asked to? Dyeing work could have been done later."

Tenali said, "There are not much dyes left and I was afraid that if I moved from there, the dyes would finish and I might not get any dyes to colour my clothes because there is a huge demand for the dyes."

"Why won't you get dyes for clothes?" asked the surprised king.

"My Lord, ever since you ordered for coloured sweets to be prepared, all the sweet sellers are buying and using clothes dye to colour their sweets," said Tenali Raman.

The king was shocked to hear this.

The king said, "What? The sweet sellers are colouring the sweets with the dyes meant for dyeing clothes!"

Tenali said, "Yes, My Lord, and if they use up all the dyes for sweets, then how will I dye my clothes for the festival."

The king said, "The dye for clothes is not fit for comsumption. It should not be used in sweets. It is bad for health."

"I know that, My Lord," said Tenali Raman.

The king then announced, "Courtiers, all of you listen. I take back the order to prepare colourful sweets and all those people who have used cloth dyes in sweets shall be punished."

Tenali Raman said, "Thank you, my Lord. This is what I wanted."

The king replied, "I should thank you, Tenali Raman. You have saved the lives of the people of our kingdom."

THE BEAUTIFUL DANCER

There were many courtiers who were jealous of Tenali Raman because the king was very fond of him.

The priest in the court was also jealous of Tenali Raman. He would often suggest hanging Tenali Raman.

But clever as he was, Tenali would always use his wit and clever thinking to get out of the difficult situation.

However, the priest would not give up and continued telling the king false stories about Tenali Raman so that the king would get angry and punish him.

Tenali got fed up with all this. He decided that he should put an end to it, once and for all.

He thought and made a plan. He went to the priest and said, "A lovely dancer wants to meet you because you are so great. Will you go, Sir?"

"Yes, of course. But where can I meet her?" asked the priest.

Tenali said, "You will have to go to the house where she is staying."

"All right," agreed the priest.

"However she is also concerned that you might get a bad name for visiting her," said Tenali.

"Then what do we do?" asked the priest.

"She has great respect for you, and has suggested that you should come to see her disguised as a woman so that no one can recognise you," said the clever Tenali Raman.

The priest was very happy and gladly agreed.

"Yes, that is a great idea. Then no one will be able to recognise me," said the priest.

The priest was unable to contain his excitement and looked forward to the meeting with the dancer.

Then Tenali went to the king and told him the same thing.

The king was also very pleased that a renowned and beautiful dancer had called him great and wanted to meet him.

He also agreed to go dressed as a woman, so that no one could recognise him and no harm would come to his honour.

Tenali had called both of them at the same house. The priest had been called ten minutes earlier than the king.

Tenali reached the house before either of them and put off the lights of the house.

The priest came first and sat down. Tenali had told them both that the lights would be off so that no one could see them.

The priest then heard the tinkle of anklets. He immediately understood that the dancer had come. The king dressed as a woman and wearing anklets on his feet, walked into the dark room.

The priest kept waiting for a while to let the beautiful dancer say something.

But the 'woman' said nothing and kept standing.

So, the priest started the conversation and said, "I have heard that you are very beautiful. Show me your face, please."

The king heard the voice of the priest and recognised it at once. He shouted, "Priest! What are you doing here?"

The priest also recognised the king's voice and asked, "My Lord, what are you doing here?"

The king asked him, "Did Tenali Raman tell you to come here?"

The priest said, "Yes, and you?"

The king shouted, "Tenali has made a fool of us. I will get him hanged."

Suddenly they heard someone locking the door from outside.

They heard Tenali say, "I thank both of you for coming here. But you will only get out of here when you promise to stop blaming me and trying to punish me with death sentence."

Both of them had no other option but to agree.

"Yes, yes we promise you. Now please open the door," they said together.

Tenali Raman opened the door and let the king and the priest go. Feeling ashamed at what had happened they returned home quickly. Tenali saw them running away and had a hearty laugh.

MILK FOR THE CATS

Once, the population of the rats in the city increased so much that everywhere there were rats. The rats were damaging the grains and were roaming around in the houses biting children.

The king issued orders for every citizen to be given a cat to kill the rats in the city. The considerate king also ordered for every household to be given a cow so as to feed their milk to the cats.

Tenali did not like the idea. He thought that there were many children who were very poor and did not get milk to drink.

Instead of providing the milk to the children, the king was asking the cow milk to be fed to the cats who were actually supposed to eat the rats.

Tenali made a plan. He was also given a cat. He gave his cat hot milk which burnt its mouth.

The cat got scared and stopped drinking milk and started eating the rats in Tenali's house.

After a few days, the king went out to survey the situation regarding the rats and to see if the cats were being looked after.

He was surprised to see the streets still full of rats. There did not seem to be any decrease in their number. Infact, there were more rats than before.

He noticed that rats moved freely in all the houses except Tenali's.

The king was surprised and said, "Tenali, why is it that there are no rats in your house while all the other houses are full of rats?"

Tenali came forward and said, "My Lord, I did not feed the cow milk to the cat in my house. Instead I deliberately gave it hot milk to scare it so that the cat would catch rats to eat. Pardon me, but cow's milk is not meant to be given to cats but to poor children. There are many poor children. They don't get milk to drink. Would it be wise to give milk to the cats instead of the children?"

The king said, "You are right Tenali. Every child should get milk to drink."

He ordered his minister, “Tell all the people to give the milk to poor and needy children and not to the cats.”

When the cats were not given any milk, they began to chase and eat the rats who were still running around. Soon there were no more rats in the kingdom.

MANGOES AND RODS

The old mother of the king became very ill. She was so sick that she left all hope of getting well again. She called the king and said, "Son, you know that I love mangoes very much. As my last wish I want you to get mangoes for me to eat."

The king loved his mother a lot. He wanted to fulfil his mother's desire but unfortunately it was not the season for mangoes. He rushed his men here and there, but no mangoes could be found anywhere.

After a few days the mother died. The king was very sad that he had not been able to fulfil his mother's last wish.

The king asked the chief priest, "How can I fulfil the last wish of my dead mother?"

The priest was a very greedy man and was always on the lookout to extract expensive gifts from the king.

He said, "You cannot get mangoes in this season. But you can compensate by giving mangoes made of gold to the priests because we priests are the messangers of the God. If you give mangoes to us, then your mother's noble soul would be very pleased and would rest in peace. She would bless you for fulfilling her last desire."

The king did the same and organised a royal feast for all the priests. In the end, he gave each priest a mango of gold.

All this while, Tenali Raman had been away. When he came back and heard about it, he decided to teach the priests a lesson.

He invited the priests for a meal saying, "I want to fulfil the last wish of my dead mother."

All the priests came because they thought that Tenali would also give them some costly gift.

Tenali Raman fed all the priests a wonderful meal. After the meal, as they waited for the costly gifts, Tenali asked his servant to light a fire and put some iron rods in that fire.

The chief priest asked, "What are you doing Tenali?"

Tenali said, "I want to fulfil my mother's last wish."

The priest said, "That is very nice. You are a good son. What was her last wish?"

Tenali said, "My mother was very sick and in great pain before she died. The last thing she wanted was that burning iron rods should be placed on her knees, so that her pain would subside."

"What!" said the priests.

Tenali said, "I could not do it then because she died soon after. Now, I want to fulfil her last wish by keeping these burning iron rods on the knees of each one of you."

Angry and scared, all the priests got up in an instant.

They shouted, “How can you do something so cruel to us?”

“I have to fulfil her last wish and that is the only way,” said Tenali.

“Who told you that her last wish would be fulfilled by doing that to us?” asked the chief priest.

“You only told the king that he could fulfil his mother’s last wish by giving each one of you a mango made of gold,” said Tenali.

The chief priest said, “We are sorry for that. You can take back those mangoes made of gold, but we cannot bear the burning rods. Please let us go.”

They all returned the gold mangoes and went away. Clever that they were, the priests went straight to the king and complained about Tenali Raman.

The king thought that Tenali had become greedy and so scolded him. He asked him to explain his misbehaviour.

Tenali said, “Not me, but the priests have become greedy.”

Tenali continued, "If they could take gold mangoes from you to fulfil your mother's last wish, why could they not take the burning iron rods to fulfil my mother's last wish?"

The king said, "You are right Tenali Raman. The priest have become very greedy. I will punish them. You can keep all the gold mangoes as a reward."

THE BLUE MAN'S FAIRIES

One day a blue skinned man came to the court of King Krishnadev Rai and said, "My respects to you, My Lord!"

A moment of silence fell over the court as all the courtiers, the guards and even the king himself stared at the blue man who indeed looked very strange.

Breaking the silence, the blue man said, "I have magical powers, My Lord. I know where the fairies live and I can call them to meet you. They would be of great help to you."

The king eagerly said, "Yes, I would surely like to see the fairies. When and where can I meet them?"

The blue man said, "You will have to go near the old water tank outside the city at midnight. You must go alone and only then can you meet the fairies when I chant the magical words to call them."

That very night, the king rode on his horse alone to the old water tank.

The water tank was next to the ruins of an old fort.

The blue man stood waiting and as he saw the king, the blue man immediately came forward to greet the king.

He said to the king, “Please, come inside the fort and I will call the fairies for you.”

Just as the king was about to enter the fort, someone clapped. Soon many soldiers belonging to the king’s own army came and stood all around them.

The king was surprised to see them there because he had not ordered the soldiers to be there.

Before the king could say anything, the soldiers arrested the blue man, who tried hard to run away, but could not.

The king, not understanding anything, shouted, “What is happening here?”

Then he heard a voice. It was the voice of Tenali Raman.

Tenali Raman said, “This man cannot show you any fairies, My Lord. He does not have magical powers.”

“Who is he then?” asked the king.

Tenali said, “He is just an ordinary man who has come here only to harm you.”

“What!” cried the king.

Tenali said, “This man is a minister from the neighbouring kingdom. The fairies inside the old fort are actually soldiers from his kingdom who have come dressed as fairies. They have hidden weapons in their wings.”

"Where are they now?" asked the king.

"We have arrested them. They had come to kill you," said Tenali.

The king said, "Oh! Tenali. Thank you for saving my life, but how did you come to know?"

"By seeing some drops of sweat on this blue man's face," said Tenali.

"I don't understand," said the king.

Tenali explained, "When this man came to the court, he was afraid that he might be caught."

"How do you know that, Tenali?" asked the king.

Tenali said, "He was sweating and I saw that the drops of sweat had removed some of the blue colour from his skin."

"Thank God you saw it, Tenali," said the king gratefully.

Tenali continued, "I did not trust this blue man and I asked my servants to follow him."

"That was smart," complemented the king.

Tenali said, "Then my servants saw him talking to the soldiers hiding in this old dry water tank."

"What happened then?" asked the king.

Tenali said, "The servants heard them planning your murder. When my servants told me, I got the soldiers to this place. The rest you know."

"Thank you, Tenali. You have been so clever," said the king.

"It was my duty, My Lord," said Tenali.

The king sat on his horse and all the soldiers, with their fairy prisoners, also went back to the court. The enemy soldiers were put in jail and ordered to be killed.

The king rewarded Tenali Raman handsomely for his clever thinking.

NEWS FROM THE COURT

The royal priest was very jealous of Tenali Raman because he was a favourite of the king.

So the royal priest always tried to get Tenali in trouble with the king.

One day, the royal priest made yet another attempt to put Tenali Raman in trouble. He said, "We should always let the general public know whatever we talk in the court. They should know what happens in the court."

The commander of the army also agreed and said, "Tenali Raman is the best person to provide this news to the public because he is the most clever of us all."

The king said, "Tenali, you will write down the proceedings of the court."

"Yes, My Lord," said Tenali.

The king added, "You will go along with a drum beater and read out the news."

Tenali knew that some jealous courtiers were trying to tease him. So, he planned to teach them all a lesson.

Every day Tenali would write and go along with the drum beater all over the city and stop at different places to loudly narrate the news of the court.

The drum beater would beat his drum and the people would come closer to him. Then Tenali Raman would read out the news written by him.

On the first day Tenali Raman announced, “This is by the order of Our Majesty that whatever happens in the court will be told to the people. It will be written and narrated by me.”

Tenali continued, “The news is as follows: Today, the king talked about a new law to punish bad people.”

All the people came closer.

Tenali said, “The king asked the royal priest about the old law but he was sleeping in the court. The king scolded him and asked him to go home and sleep.”

On the second day, Tenali said, “Today the great commander of our army came in late and the king became red with anger. More about it tomorrow.”

Tenali made the people laugh at the priest and the commander of the army because he knew that these two envied him a lot.

The people really enjoyed what Tenali wrote and every day a large number of people would gather to hear the news of the court.

The people would burst out laughing when Tenali made fun of the royal priest and the army commander, since very few people in the kingdom liked them.

The friends and the servants of the royal priest and the army commander would come and tell them how Tenali Raman's news was damaging their reputation.

Now both of them were worried that they had become the laughing stock for everyone.

The commander said to the priest, "We were trying to hurt Tenali but he is hurting us. Please do something, royal priest."

The priest said, "Let me see. I shall try to convince the king to stop the news of the court from being read outside."

Next day, the priest went to the king and said, "My Lord, I first thought that reading the court news in public would be a good idea."

"On second thoughts, I feel that the proceedings of the court should not be told to the people. This news reading in public should be stopped immediately."

Tenali said, "You should have actually had your second thoughts first. Then you should have thrown your first thoughts into the rubbish can."

Everyone started laughing and the priest hung his head in shame.

IS ANYONE CONTENT?

One day, the king looked at Tenali and said, "You are not the same as you were. You look different."

"How, My Lord?" asked Tenali Raman.

The king said, "You are wearing fine clothes and jewels. Earlier you wore very simple clothes."

Tenali said, "It is all due to your kindness, My Lord. I have saved a little and so am better off now. Me and my family are very happy."

The king said, "If you have a lot, you should share it with others."

Tenali replied, "I have always been very poor. I have not saved so much that I can give to others also."

"No, no. You should at least give something to the others," said the king.

Tenali said, "I have suffered a lot. After I enjoy my riches for sometime, I promise that I will give to others too, My Lord."

But the king insisted, "No, Tenali. You have to donate something."

Realising that the king would not listen, Tenali asked, "What do you want me to do, My Lord?"

The king replied, "Construct a big house with your money and then gift it to someone."

"But why shouldn't I live in that house, My Lord? I also want my wife and my children to live in a big house," said Tenali.

The king said, "No, it is my order. Also, gifting the house to someone will give you happiness and contentment."

"As you say, My Lord," said Tenali, not really happy with the idea.

So Tenali started to construct a grand house. He got it ready within a few months. The house was big and strong.

When the house was ready, Tenali put up a board outside it which read, "This house will be given as a gift to any man who is happy and content with what he has."

Many people came, saw the house and really liked it. Everyone wanted the house but none said that he was happy and content with what he already had.

One day a poor man, from another city, happened to read the board.

He went to Tenali and said, "I have read the board put up outside the house. I am happy and content with what I have. So I think that I am the right person to have this house."

"If you are happy and content, then why do you need this house?" said Tenali.

The poor man had no answer, and so he went away. Tenali went and told the story to the king.

The king said, "You have been very clever again."

Tenali said, "My Lord! I would have definitely given away the house to someone who was content with his life. But everyone wants more and more, no matter how much they already have."

"So what are you going to do now?" asked the king.

Tenali said, "Since I could find no one who deserved this house, I think I will move into the house myself along with my family."

The king smiled and said, "It was very clever of you to put up that board outside the house. You knew that no one is ever content and everyone yearns for more and more. You made sure Tenali, that none but only you, could own the house."

"My Lord, I cannot help being clever," said Tenali smiling.

Tenali went home and told his family that they would live in the new house.

The family was very happy to move into the big house where they lived happily together.

TENALI AND THE WRESTLER

One day, a wrestler came from a neighbouring kingdom and challenged the people to wrestle with him

The wrestler had a well built body. The kingdom's strongest wrestlers fought with him but were all defeated badly.

King Krishnadev Rai got very annoyed and said to the commander of the army, "You mean to say that there is no one in my kingdom who is strong and brave enough to fight with this wrestler?"

The commander said, "This wrestler is very strong and huge. No one can defeat him."

King Krishnadev Rai said, "He is challenging everyone to fight with him. The honour of our kingdom is at stake, and if no one can defeat him then the whole world will ridicule us."

All the courtiers kept quiet as they had seen the huge wrestler walking along the streets challenging people, "Come on, fight with me. You are cowards."

The king asked, "Is there no one who can save the honour of our kingdom?"

Finally Tenali said, "My Lord, I will fight the wrestler."

Everyone thought of it as a joke and started laughing.

Tenali ignored them and said, "Someone has to guard the honour of our kingdom. I will fight with the wrestler."

The royal priest said, "This is not child's play. Have you seen that wrestler? He is very strong. Even our strongest men could not defeat him."

Tenali said, "Yes, I have seen him and I did not like the way he was making fun of everyone and calling us all cowards. I will wrestle with him."

The priest said, "He will break your bones."

Tenali said, "We will see who will break whose bones."

The king warned Tenali, "This will not be easy. Don't do it."

But as Tenali was adamant, the king had to agree.

The word spread that Tenali was to fight with that strong and huge wrestler.

The wrestler also came to know about it and when he saw the small Tenali, he burst out laughing.

He went on laughing and laughing, till he rolled on the floor.

Tenali went away from there. Then he sent one of his men to the wrestler.

The man went to the wrestler and said, “Don’t think that Tenali is weak. The demons of war have blessed him with extraordinary powers.”

The wrestler got worried and asked the man to show him the demon.

The man said, “Come with me.”

The man took the wrestler to an old temple near the river. There they saw a huge shadow with horns, standing right behind Tenali.

The stupid wrestler did not realise that the demon was nothing but Tenali's own shadow.

The wrestler asked, "Who is that?"

"That is the demon of war blessing Tenali with special powers. You would certainly be a very brave man if you still want to fight Tenali, who has such great powers. If I were in your place, I would never fight him."

The wrestler said, "What would you do then?"

The man said, "I would run away."

The wrestler looked at the huge shadow again and said, "You are right. I will also go away. Don't tell anyone. I will leave right away."

The wrestler packed up his belongings and left the city immediately.

Next day when the soldiers went to call the wrestler for the fight with Tenali, the wrestler was not there. They went back to inform the king.

Everyone was present in the court when the soldiers told the king that the wrestler had run away.

The king looked at Tenali and said, “Did you cast some kind of a magic spell on him? I am sure that you have made him leave the city and go away.”

Tenali smiled and narrated the whole story. Everyone burst out laughing.

WHAT KILLED THE GOAT?

King Krishnadev Rai looked surprisingly at the man who was crying aloud, "My Lord, My Lord! Please help me."

The king asked, "What is the matter?"

The man said, "I am a shepherd. I had a goat. It died yesterday because it got crushed under the wall of my old neighbour's house."

"So how can we help you?" asked one of the courtiers.

The man said, "The walls of the old man's house are not strong enough."

"So you think it is the old man's fault?" asked Tenali.

"Yes, and he should give me money because my goat died under his wall."

Tenali said, "My Lord, I don't think that the old man needs to give money. He is not to be blamed."

"Then who is to be blamed?" asked the king.

"I will find out," said Tenali.

Tenali called the old man to the court and asked him to pay the shepherd for his goat.

The old man said, "I am not to be blamed for the falling of the wall. It was not strong enough, so it fell."

"Who was the mason who built the wall? Call him," said Tenali at once.

The mason came but he said, "It is not my fault. I made the wall with the cement given to me by a helper. Take the money from him."

The helper was called and he said, "I am not to be blamed, sir. The waterman put more water than was needed. He should be held responsible."

The waterman was summoned. He said, "Spare me Sir, it is not my fault. The opening of my goat's skin water bag is very big. So more water flows out of it. What can I do?"

"Who gave you the goat skin?" asked the king.

"This shepherd gave it to me," said the waterman.

Tenali then said to the shepherd, "You came to ask for money. Now it is proved that it was your mistake which led to the falling of the wall and caused your goat's death."

The shepherd left the court with his head hung low.

The king praised Tenali and said, "That was good thinking, Tenali. You are indeed very clever."

THE RARE BOOK

Once a very learned scholar came to the court of King Krishnadev Rai. Tenali Raman was not present that day.

The scholar said to the king, "I have spent my whole life reading and collecting knowledge. I think that I am the best. Is there anyone in your kingdom better than me?"

The king asked, "How can you be so sure?"

The scholar said, "I can discuss any topic. Let anyone come and try to defeat me in knowledge."

All the prominent scholars of the kingdom knew that the scholar was really very well read. They had no chance to defeat him.

However, since their king ordered them to discuss with the scholar, they had no choice. No matter what subject they tried to discuss with the learned scholar, he always won. Seeing no other way out, Tenali Raman was called for help.

The courtiers told him that there was no one able enough to defeat the scholar.

Tenali said, "Fix a day for a meeting to discuss a book."

On the fixed day Tenali Raman came dressed as a scholar priest. He held a bundle under his arm.

The king came and took his place. Tenali bowed to the king and sat down on one of the chairs kept in front of the king.

Tenali kept the bundle on the table between the two chairs. The scholar came and sat on the opposite chair.

The king said, "Now the debate can be started."

Tenali Raman greeted the scholar and said to him, "We all know that you are a very learned scholar. I have brought a very rare and great book about which we shall discuss today."

The scholar said, "Tell me the name of the book. There is no book which I have not read. I am sure I will know it."

Tenali said, “The name of the book is ‘Tilakashta Mahisha Bandhana’. Now we can talk about it. Are you ready, Sir?”

The scholar had never heard of such a book in his life, but he said, “Of course. This is a great and uncommon book.”

Tenali said, “Come on, let us talk.”

Not wanting to be defeated in the discussion, the scholar said, "But I had read it a long time ago."

"Oh, I see," said Tenali.

The scholar said, "Let me read it tonight, then we will discuss tomorrow."

"All right, Sir," Tenali agreed.

The man got up and walked away.

Now the king and other courtiers were worried that the scholar would read the book and win the discussion next day.

But Tenali was not worried. He smiled and left the court.

To everyone's utter amazement, the scholar did not come the next day. The guards informed the king that the scholar had disappeared from the city at night.

The king was very surprised. He said, "Tenali, let us know about the book that you were going to talk about."

"There was no book, My Lord. 'Tilakashta' means dried sticks of sesame. 'Mahisha bandhana' means a rope."

"What?" said the king.

"The bundle I was carrying was of dried sticks of sesame tied with a rope. I covered them with silk so they looked like a book."

Nobody could hold their laughter when they found out how Tenali had fooled the scholar.

A DOG'S CURLED TAIL

The rivalry between Tenali Raman and the royal priest continued as before.

One day the priest went to the court and said to the king, "My Lord, we have heard that Tenali Raman has learnt to make a magic stone which turns iron into gold."

The king said, "Tenali should have told me about it. This stone will help me add wealth to the royal treasury."

The king sent his guards to bring Tenali to the court. When Tenali came, he bowed before the king and said, "Yes, My Lord."

The king said, "I have heard that you can make a stone that can change iron into gold. Is that true?"

Tenali at once realised that this must be the work of his enemies. He did not say anything and kept quiet.

The king asked again, "Have you made a stone like that?"

Tenali replied, "Yes, My Lord, I have."

The king ordered, "Show it to me just now."

Tenali said, "Definitely, My Lord, but it will take some time. I will show it to you tomorrow morning."

The priest was happy that he had, at last succeeded in getting Tenali into trouble.

Next day Tenali came to the court with a dog whose tail had been put in a pipe.

Everyone laughed but the king was very angry and shouted, "What is this, Tenali? What kind of a joke is this? How dare you bring a dog into the court."

Tenali said, "I want to ask you a question, My Lord."

"What is the question?" said the king.

Tenali said, "Will this dog's tail ever become straight by putting it into a pipe like this?"

The king said, "What a stupid thing to ask. No, it will never be straight. It will never change for the dog is born with a curled tail."

Tenali said, "In the same way, My Lord, iron will never change into gold."

The king realised what Tenali was trying to say. He realised that he should not have believed the royal priest.

The king knew that if Tenali was given a reward for his intelligence, the priest would feel bad.

So, he said, "You are right. For this you will get a reward."

The priest felt bad that the clever Tenali had again shown him down and was getting a reward, instead of a scolding from the king.

STRAIGHTEN THE TAIL

Everyone looked eagerly at the dog with its tail in a pipe.

Tenali removed the pipe from the dog's tail and the tail curled up as before.

As Tenali was taking the dog out of the court, a courtier said. "Our nature is like a dog's tail. It will never change."

Another said, "It may change under pressure for a long time."

The king said, "So you mean to say that if we can straighten a dog's tail then we can change our nature also."

The courtier said, “Why don’t we try it out, My Lord?”

The king agreed, “Yes, that is a nice idea.”

The king announced that ten people would be given a dog each for six months. They would all try and somehow straighten the tails of the dogs given to them. Each of them would be given ten gold coins every month to take care of the dog.

To select the ten, every courtier’s name was written on chits and ten chits were randomly picked up.

The chit with Tenali’s name was also one of the ten chits that were picked up.

Dogs were brought and given to the ten courtiers including Tenali.

For six months, the courtiers tried different ways to straighten the tail of the dog.

One courtier gave his dog a lot to eat so that its tail would become thick and because of the extra flesh it might become straight.

Another tied wooden stick supports to the dog's tail.

Someone put heavy weight on the tail, some tried to do it with magic.

Tenali did something else. He did not give the dog enough to eat for he knew that when the dog becomes weak, the tail would become limp.

After six months all the ten courtiers brought their dogs to the court.

The king noticed that none of the dogs, except for Tenali Raman's, had a straight tail.

His dog had a straight tail because it was so weak that it could not move its tail at all.

Tenali said, "See, My Lord. I have made the tail of the dog straight."

But the king got very angry seeing the weak dog.

He shouted at Tenali and said, "You are a bad man. You have not given the dog enough to eat. Look how weak it has become."

"We should be kind to animals. You have been very unkind," he added.

"But the tail is straight, My Lord," said Tenali.

"No. This is not right. This test was for healthy dogs. You have nearly killed the dog."

The priest said, “So we can say that whatever happens, our nature never changes.”

“What do you mean?” said the king.

The priest said, “We men are so greedy. We don’t change. For greed, even Tenali became cruel to the dog.”

“That is right,” said another courtier.

The priest said, “My Lord. Tenali Raman kept the ten gold coins you gave him every month for himself, and the poor dog remained hungry.”

The king nodded and then said, “The royal priest is right. You are wrong, Tenali. You have not proven anything. You have treated the poor dog very badly and you should be punished for it. You have wronged by ill treating an animal just to prove your point.”

For the first time the priest won and Tenali was scolded for treating the dog so badly.

Tenali apologised to the king for being cruel to the dog.

The king then turned to his courtiers and said, "In a way, we all are wrong including me. Each one of you tried to straighten the dog's tail one way or the other, and thus hurt the dogs. We, humans should be kind to animals and not ill treat them. From now onwards, anyone found ill treating any animal, would be severely dealt with."

THE DAILY BEATINGS

There lived a woman in a village who was very cruel to her husband. Every day she used to beat him up several times with her shoe to make him obey her.

The timid husband was so scared of her that he never said anything. He lived his life the way his wife liked.

This woman had a young daughter. No one wanted to marry the daughter because of her mother's bad nature.

The enemies of Tenali Raman saw a good opportunity and wanted to get him married to the girl to make his life miserable.

They sent a proposal to Tenali through a messanger.

He said, "I have brought a marriage proposal for you, please marry this pretty girl."

Tenali said, "I am already married and I don't want to marry a second time."

The man requested again, "Please marry her."

Tenali said, "I can't marry her but I can get her married to my younger brother."

The enemies of Tenali went to the woman and convinced her to marry her daughter to Tenali Raman's brother.

The woman agreed and the wedding date was fixed.

Now there was only one problem for Tenali Raman. He had no younger brother!

As Tenali was trying to find out a solution to this problem, he met a young man in search of a job.

Immediately an idea came to Tenali's clever mind.

He said to the young man, "If you pretend to be my younger brother and marry the girl that I tell you to, then I can get you a job at once."

The young man agreed. He was married to the girl and Tenali got him a job.

After the marriage, when the girl was ready to go to her husband's house her mother stopped her, and said, "Take this shoe. I used to hit your father several times daily with this shoe and that is why he always listen to me. You should also hit your husband many times a day. Then he will obey you."

The woman sent the father with the daughter so that she would settle down quickly and well.

Tenali had already told the young man how to control the girl, but the girl was very clever and soon started beating her husband every day, just as her mother had asked her to.

One day Tenali saw that the young man bore some blue marks on his body. When asked the young man confessed that he was beaten every day by his wife.

After sometime the girl went back, along with her father, to visit her mother.

During this period Tenali made a plan.

He made the boy exercise and learn art of self defense. He fed the young man a very good diet.

Now the young man had become strong and brave. He was no longer timid and afraid.

Tenali drilled it in mind that he should not let his wife beat him.

The training soon came to be tested.

One day a letter arrived that the wife of the young man was returning back home.

Tenali saw the face of the young man. He seemed a bit afraid. Tenali encouraged him and told him not to worry.

The wife came back. Now Tenali was eager to see the results of his training.

The first day itself the wife tried to pick up her shoe to beat her husband.

Tenali was anxiously watching from behind the window. He wanted to know whether his training was useful or not.

As the girl bent down to pick her shoe up, the young man quickly picked up a stick.

The girl lifted her hand to hit. But before she could beat him, the young man defended himself with the stick.

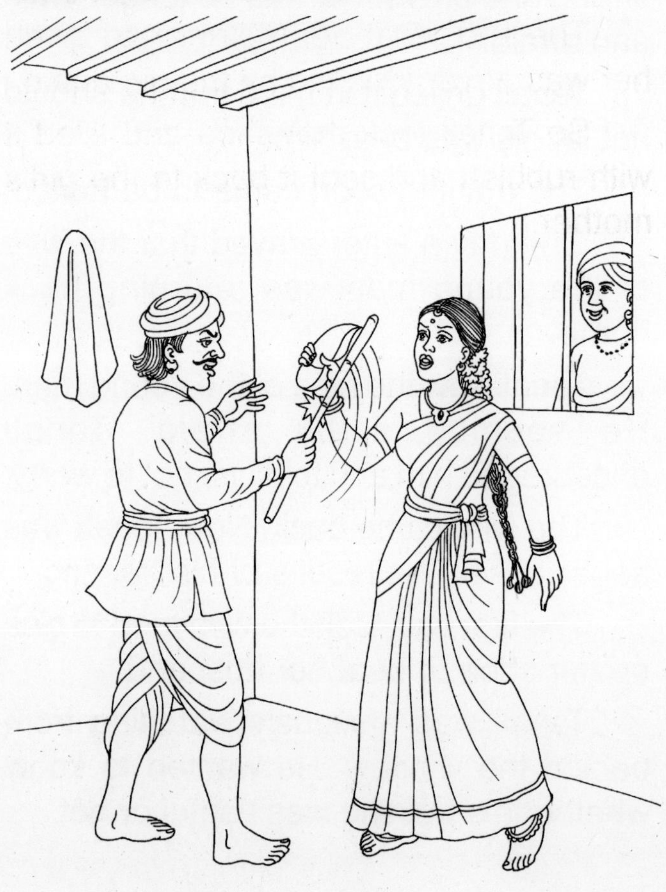

Then he hit her so hard with the stick that her hand got fractured and she screamed aloud in pain.

It took her hand some months to become all right. When she became well, she never dared to hit her husband again.

The shoe that her mother had given her was never touched by the girl again.

So Tenali took that shoe and filled it with rubbish and sent it back to the girl's mother.

NEITHER THIS NOR THAT

Once, the king became angry with a minister. He ordered him to be put in prison and forgot about it. The minister remained in prison for a long time.

Once while inspecting the prison, the king saw the minister behind the bars.

The minister was quietly sitting in a corner of his cell. He looked very weak and unhappy.

The king felt very sorry for him. He went forward and tried to talk to the minister but the minister would not reply.

The king shouted, "Why don't you talk to me?"

When the minister did not reply, the king said to the minister, "If you want to be free from the prison then you have to do one thing."

The minister spoke, "And what would that be, My Lord?"

The king said, "Ah, now you are talking."

The minister said again, "What do I have to do to be free from this prison, My Lord?"

The king said, "You will be set free on one condition. You must bring me a horse."

The minister said happily, "A horse? That would be very easy to do."

His happiness was however short-lived for the king said, "But the horse should be neither black, nor brown nor grey nor white."

"Where will I get such a horse from? But first I must get out of this prison," thought the minister.

He said aloud, "My Lord, if you free me from this prison, then I will bring the horse for you."

The king asked the guards to let the minister go, but said, "You have only one month to get the horse for me."

The minister stepped outside the prison and felt good in the open air. He felt nice that he was free, but he had only one month to bring the horse to the king.

So, he hurried out and first of all he went to Tenali Raman who knew that the minister was an honest and a good man.

The minister told his story and said, "Please help me, Tenali."

Tenali said, "Don't worry, you have a full month's time. Go back to your family. They must be missing you a lot."

"But I have to hunt for the horse. That will take time," said the worried minister.

Tenali said, "You have enough time. Trust me. When the time comes I will tell you what to do."

The minister went to his house and met his wife and children. They were very happy to see him back.

The family lived happily for a month because they were sure that Tenali would certainly find a way out.

On the last day of the month, Tenali came to see the minister and talked with him for some time.

The next day the minister went to the court. Tenali was also sitting in the court.

The king said to the minister, "What? Haven't you brought the horse for me?"

The minister said, "I have got the horse you wanted, My Lord. Please send a man to my house to fetch it."

"When should I send the man?" asked the king.

The minister replied, "My Lord, you can send the man any day, only it should not be a Sunday or Monday, nor a Tuesday.... or Wednesday, nor Thursday nor Friday ..... or Saturday. Any other day would be just fine."

The king was quite for a while and then laughing out aloud, he said to the minister, "Tell me honestly. Whose advice did you seek on the matter?"

The minister answered, "My Lord, Tenali Raman."

The king turned to Tenali and said, "So Tenali, you have yet again used your intelligence to help a person in trouble."

Tenali bowed before the king. The minister was again appointed on his previous post.

The minister thanked Tenali for his help.

TENALI'S MOUSTACHE

The king was in his court with all his courtiers when a guard came and said, "My Lord, there are many people gathered outside who are crying and want to see you."

"Tenali, go and find out what the matter is," said the worried king.

Tenali came back after some time and informed the king, "There have been many cases of theft all over the kingdom. The people are very upset."

The king got even more worried and summoned the army commander.

The commander came and said, "I have been trying to solve this problem for a long time but the robbers are very clever and so have not yet been caught."

The king ordered more guards to be put on duty round the clock, to ensure the safety of his people and their belongings.

The vigilant guards did everything they could, but the thefts continued.

Angry and upset, the king shouted at the commander, saying, "What do you want me to do? Should I hand over the kingdom to the robbers?"

The king said in despair, "Is there no way that these robbers can be caught so that my people can live in peace as before?"

The commander said, “These robbers are from the neighbouring kingdom. Their leader is very clever.”

The king turned to Tenali and said, “Can you stop these robberies?”

Tenali said, "Just give me your command, and I will get the whole gang and the gang leader here in a sack, in a few days time."

"If you do that, then I will reward you handsomely," said the king.

Tenali said, "Yes, My Lord."

Tenali took the king's leave and went back home, all along thinking of a plan.

Tenali told his men to go and tell the people that Tenali was trying to learn black magic to deal with the gang leader.

As planned, the men went and started telling everyone that Tenali had shifted to a new house and was chanting secret mantras to learn black magic.

Soon the rumour spread and people started talking about it.

The gang leader too came to know about it.

The gang leader thought, "I would like to see what this man is doing. No one can catch me. I must teach him a lesson."

Tenali's loyal men were spread all over the city to find out if there were any strangers in the city.

One of Tenali's men overheard a man say, "If the gang leader finds Tenali, he shall pull out his moustache."

The servant thought, "This man does not know that Tenali does not have a moustache. He appears to be new here. I must follow him."

The servant tried to follow the stranger but soon lost him in the dark of the night. He went and told Tenali about this, who told him not to worry.

After some time, a holy man came to the house where Tenali had been staying for the last one month.

The holy man was actually the gang leader. He started begging loudly outside Tenali's house.

A voice came from inside, "I cannot open the door."

The gang leader said, "I am a holy man. You have to give me something."

The voice said, “Oh! But I am busy learning black magic to catch the robbers. All right come to the window and I will give you something.”

The gang leader went near the window. The window opened slowly and a face appeared before him.

It was Tenali Raman sporting a huge long and bushy moustache. Tenali peeped from the window to give the holy man something to eat.

As his moustache touched the window grill, the gang leader, disguised as the holy man, grabbed the moustache and pulled it off from Tenali's face and said loudly, "I am the gang leader. Now catch me if you can!"

As he said this, one of Tenali's strongman, who had been hiding all this while, came out from the hiding and hit the gang leader hard on the head with a stick.

The gang leader fell down unconscious. Tenali's man brought a big sack and put the gang leader into the sack. The sack, with the gang leader in it was taken to the court.

Tenali entered the court, wearing the moustache again, followed by his servants with the sack.

The sack was shaking a lot and making a lot of noise because the gang leader had regained consciousness and was screaming and trying to free himself from the sack.

The sack was untied in front of the whole court. As the gang leader came out of it, he was immediately arrested by the soldiers.

He begged for mercy but was taken to the prison.

The king was very happy with Tenali.

He asked, "Tenali, this is your best work till now. Tell us, how did you catch this very strong, clever and cruel gang leader?"

Tenali said, "My men spread the rumour that I was learning black magic to catch the robbers. One of my men heard a stranger saying that the gang leader would pull out my moustache if he meets me. I availed this opportunity, and wore a false moustache. When the gang leader came to my house, my man hit him with a stick."

The priest asked, "But how did he know your whereabouts?"

Tenali said, "My men spread the news that I was living in that house to learn black magic."

A courtier got up and said, "I must admit that Tenali Raman, you have done very well."

Tenali said, "Thank you , Sir."

The king said, "Yes and now that the leader has been caught, the others would be caught too."

Tenali said, "My clever men have already caught the other gang members."

The king said, "Tenali you will get a handsome reward as I had promised."

Tenali said, "My Lord, my men have worked day and night. They have really helped me."

The king said, "Tenali, your men will also be rewarded. Please call them here and I shall reward them personally."

Tenali's men were very happy and appreciated the fact that Tenali had told the king about their contribution.

They all thanked Tenali, and for the first time the royal priest got up and said, "Tenali Raman, you are great. May God bless you."